Ups and Downs with OINK and PEARL

Kay Chorao

Harper & Row, Publishers

Ups and Downs with Oink and Pearl

10 9 8 7 6 5 4 3 2 1
First Edition

Library of Congress Cataloging-in-Publication Data
Chorao, Kay.
Ups and downs with Oink and Pearl.

(An I can read book)
Summary: Piglet Oink concocts an unusual birthday present for his sister Pearl, helps her escape from a witch, and ignores her advice on a mail-order movie projector.
[1. Pigs—Fiction. 2. Brothers and sisters—Fiction] I. Title. II. Series
PZ7.C4463Up 1986 [E] 85-45264
ISBN 0-06-021274-8
ISBN 0-06-021275-6 (lib. bdg.)

E
C

Contents

1

Super-Fizz Soda

"There is something special
about today," Oink said.
He rolled out of bed
and ran into Pearl's room.
Pearl was asleep,
but there was a card
at the foot of her bed.

It said:

HAPPY BIRTHDAY
LOVE,
MOMMA and POPPA
P.S. Enjoy your jogging suit!

"Oh, no," cried Oink.

"The something special

is Pearl's birthday."

Oink scratched his ear.

"What will I give her?"

He watched the sun rise.

It looked like a ball of

ice cream.

"That is it!" cried Oink.

He jumped up and down.

"I will make

a super-fizz ice-cream soda

for Pearl!"

Oink ran down to the kitchen.

He opened the refrigerator.

"Good, we have ice cream,"

he said.

It was banana crunch.

"Now I need a big glass,

and soda water,

and syrup, and...."

“Hi,” said Pearl.

“I am going jogging.”

She ran out the back door.

"Pearl will get hot jogging.
A super-fizz soda will be
a perfect birthday present,"
said Oink.
He got a tall glass
and dropped a giant scoop
of ice cream into it.
Plop!

Oink looked for soda water.

He looked everywhere.

At last he found a box.

It said BAKING SODA.

"Good," said Oink.

He poured it into the glass.

Then he added lemon juice.

"Hooray!" cried Oink.

"It fizzes!"

It fizzed and fizzed,

all over the table.

He put chocolate syrup,

gooseberry jam, baking soda,

a cherry, and

still more baking soda

into the glass.

"Now it is perfect," Oink said.

Pearl was still jogging.

She was feeling hotter and hotter.

"I am so thirsty

I could drink a whole lake,"

she said.

She ran into the house.

“Water! Water!” Pearl cried.
She grabbed the super-fizz soda
and gulped down a giant swallow.

"Happy birthday, Pearl,"

sang Oink.

"UGH!" yelled Pearl.

She grabbed her throat

and ran to the sink.

She gulped water.

"That is the worst thing

I have ever tasted.

It is lumpy and horrid.

Did you put salt in it?"

"No," said Oink,

"I put in baking soda

to make fizz."

Tears came to Oink's eyes.

"I tried hard to make

a super-fizz soda

for your birthday, Pearl."

"Baking soda is for baking,"
said Pearl.
"It makes cakes pop up.
It tastes like salt."
"Oh," said Oink.
Oink tasted the super-fizz soda.
"UGH!" he cried.
Pearl started to laugh.
Oink looked at her
and started to laugh, too.
Soon there were tears
rolling down their cheeks.

"You made a terrible super-fizz
birthday soda," said Pearl,
"but you gave me
a good birthday laugh!"

2

Magic Movie Toy

Every morning,
Oink ate Monster Munch Cereal.
Some days
he ate two bowls of it.
"How can you eat that stuff?"
asked Pearl.
"It gives muscles," said Oink.
"It gives holes in your teeth,"
said Pearl.

"For three box tops and $1.50
it gives you a magic movie toy,"
said Oink.
"Let me see," said Pearl.
She grabbed the cereal box.

It showed a red projector

with a yellow handle.

"Humph," said Pearl.

"Plastic! It must be junk."

Oink ate another bowl of Munch.

After days and days
of eating Monster Munch,
Oink finished three boxes.
He put three box tops
and one dollar and fifty cents
into an envelope.
He mailed the envelope
to the Monster Munch Company.
Two weeks passed.
The mailman came
but nothing came for Oink.
Three weeks passed.
Still nothing.

Five weeks passed.

Still nothing.

"The Monster Munch Company
fooled you," said Pearl.
"They did not," said Oink.
"You will see."
"I do see," said Pearl.
"I see you have no money,
and no movie toy."
"I have lots of money," said Oink.
He shook his kitty bank.
Six pennies bounced out.
"See!" said Oink.
Pearl did not say anything,
she just walked away.

Oink piled the pennies.

It was a small pile.

"Maybe Pearl is right," he said.

He felt sad.

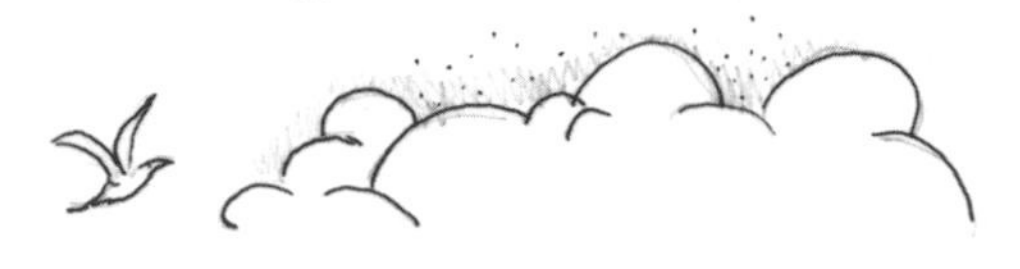

Oink walked to the mailbox.

He looked inside.

A box!

Oink grabbed it and

tore it open.

"Hooray! Yippee!

My movie set!" he yelled.

Nellie and Agnes came over to look.

But not Pearl.

"Oooooo," cried Agnes.

"A movie machine," said Nellie.

“Can we see the movie?”

asked Agnes.

“Please!” said Nellie.

Oink felt important.

He marched into the house.

Agnes and Nellie followed him.

But not Pearl.

“It will not work,” said Pearl.

“Then don’t come,” said Oink.

He led Agnes and Nellie

into the hall closet

and shut the door.

Agnes and Nellie and Oink
giggled and laughed
in the dark.
Pearl listened outside the door.
"Oooooo, it works," cried Nellie.
"Of course," said Oink.
"Look at the flying dog,"
yelled Agnes.
"Wow!" cried Nellie.
Pearl frowned.
"Who cares about flying dogs,"
she said.
Nobody heard her.

"Look out for the worm!"

squealed Agnes.

"Eeeeeek!"

yelled Nellie and Agnes together.

"Look at the monster cockroach!"

yelled Oink.

"Yuck."

"Eeeeeeeeek."

"Help!"

"The cockroach is eating the dog!"

yelled Nellie.

They hooted and laughed.

Pearl could hear them
giggling and laughing.

Pearl opened the door a crack.
"Shut the door," yelled Agnes.
Pearl turned away.

Pearl rushed upstairs.

Tears ran down her face.

“I thought Nellie and Agnes

were *my* friends, not Oink’s.

But they hate me,” Pearl cried.

“Even Oink hates me.”

Pearl buried her face
in the pillow.
She did not hear Oink come
into her room.

"Why are you crying?"

asked Oink.

"Go away," said Pearl.

"You would not let me

see the movie."

"You said it was junk,"

said Oink.

"I was wrong," said Pearl,

"you had fun."

"You were not *all* wrong,"

said Oink.

Pearl sat up.

"I was not?" she asked.

"The movie is fun," said Oink.

"But the machine does not plug in.

You have to turn the handle."

Oink rubbed his arm.

"My arm is almost falling off,"

he said.

Pearl smiled.

"Can I see the movie

if *I* turn the handle?"

Pearl asked.

"Yes," said Oink.

They ran to the closet

and watched the movie.

They giggled
and they laughed
all by themselves
in the dark.

3

Witch

Oink and Pearl
watched some ants
carrying cookie crumbs.
"This is boring," said Pearl.
"I like ants," said Oink.
"I want to do something exciting,"
said Pearl.
"Let's go to the witch's house."

Oink sat up.

“No, Pearl.

I will not go there again!

Remember on Halloween,

when I knocked

on the witch’s door?

She yelled,

‘GET OUT, LITTLE PIG,

OR I WILL BOIL YOU WITH ONIONS!’

She had a spoon in her hand.

It was dripping something red."

"But I told you it was tomato sauce,"

said Pearl.

"But *I* know it was blood,"

said Oink.

"*You* go and visit the witch.

I will stay and watch ants."

Pearl stood up.

"Come on, Oink.

It will be fun."

"NO!" cried Oink.

"Well, I am going," said Pearl.

Oink watched Pearl run
toward the witch's house.
It had towers like lizards.
It had scary faces on the walls.

It had windows

like bug eyes.

There was a fence with points

all around the house.

Oink thought about Pearl

inside that house.

"Pearl is a little fat," he said.

"She would taste good to a witch."

Oink could see Pearl

in a pot, with onions.

Lots of onions!

Oink was scared.

He ran!

He squeezed through the fence

and ran to a window.

But the window was high up.

Oink climbed into a bush
and pulled himself higher
and higher.
Up and up he climbed
until he reached the window.
He looked inside.
Nobody was there!
But the table was set with
a witch spoon,
a witch fork, and
a sharp witch knife.

Oink sniffed the air.

"Oh, no!" he cried. "Onions!

Pearl stew!"

He heard footsteps.

THE WITCH!

"Help!" cried Oink.

Oink fell.

Bump.

Bump.

Bump.

Oink fell down,

down,

down,

and landed with a crash.

“Run, Oink!” yelled a voice.

Oink ran!

It was Pearl.

She grabbed him and

pulled him through the fence.

"GET OUT AND STAY OUT!"

yelled the witch.

Oink and Pearl did not stop running
until they got to their own yard.

"How did you get away
from the witch?" asked Oink.
"She never saw me.
I only peeked at her
through the fence," said Pearl.

"I thought she was *eating* you,"

said Oink.

"I was really scared."

"Were you scared

that something awful

was happening to *me*?" asked Pearl.

Oink rubbed his ear
and looked away.
Pearl gave him a hug.

"Want an ice-cream cone?"
she asked.
Oink nodded.

"What flavor?" she asked.

"Anything but onion," said Oink.

They went to the ice-cream store.

Pearl bought Oink
a chocolate double-decker cone
with sprinkles.
His favorite.